P9-EEU-588

TONY HAWK'S 900 revolution

VOLUME 3

Tony Hawk's 900 Revolution
is published by Stone Arch Books
a Capstone imprint, 151 Good Counsel Drive, P.O. Box 669
Mankato, Minnesota 56002 www.capstonepub.com

Copyright © 2012 by Stone Arch Books All rights reserved.
No part of this publication may be reproduced in whole
or in part, or stored in a retrieval system, or transmitted
in any form or by any means, electronic, mechanical,
photocopying, recording, or otherwise, without written
permission of the publisher.

Cataloging-in-Publication Data is available on the Library
of Congress website.
ISBN: 978-1-4342-3204-5 (library binding)
ISBN: 978-1-4342-3453-7 (paperback)

Summary: Amy Kestrel is a powder pig. Often hidden
beneath five layers of hoodies, this CO ski bum is tough
to spot on the street. However, get her on the slopes,
and she's hard to miss. Amy always has the latest and
greatest gear. But when a group of masked men threaten
her mountain, she'll need every ounce of the one thing she
lacks — confidence — and only the Revolution can help
her find it.

Photo and Vector Graphics Credits: Shutterstock.
Photo credit page 122, Bart Jones/ Tony Hawk.
Photo credit page 123, Zachary Sherman

Flip Animation Illustrator: Thomas Emery
Colorist: Leonardo Lto

Creative Director: Heather Kindseth
Cover and Interior Graphic Designer: Kay Fraser
Comic Insert Graphic Designer: Brann Garvey
Production Specialist: Michelle Biedscheid

Printed in the United States of America in Stevens Point,
Wisconsin.

032011
006111WZF11

TONY HAWK'S 900 revolution

FALL LINE

BY M. ZACHARY SHERMAN // ILLUSTRATED BY CAIO MAJADO

VOLUME 3

STONE ARCH BOOKS
a capstone imprint

BOCA RATON PUBLIC LIBRARY
BOCA RATON, FLORIDA

ON JULY 27, 1999 . . .

TONY HAWK LANDED THE FIRST-EVER 900.

1

"You don't have to do this, you know?" the boy said staring into his friend's nervous eyes.

"Yes, I do," she said, swallowing hard. "My mom always says, 'It's not our successes that make us who we are; it's our failures that define us.'"

"Fine," the boy replied. "I get it. But do you need to *fail* in front of all these people?"

"Thanks for the vote of confidence, Jimmy," the girl said. She turned away from her friend. The cold air briskly whipped across her face, and her blood ran cold.

Amy Kestrel finally noticed the large crowd that had gathered around them. Five of her freshman classmates, seven older boys from school, her brother Mark, and, of course, one snow rescue paramedic.

Amy was about to take on the Falcon run at the Arapahoe Basin Ski Area on the Continental Divide in Summit County, Colorado. She swallowed hard, smiled a bit, and gave the crowd a sheepish wave. Then, Amy gave one last look at her friend, Jimmy.

"When did they all get here?" she asked.

"Thirty minutes ago!" Jimmy shot back. "As long as you've been staring down at this mountain."

Amy took another look. This wasn't the bunny slope or even a beginner's trail. Falcon was a vicious double black diamond. Only the best snowboarders in the county would dare take the run.

"Amy," Jimmy said. "You don't need to prove anything to anyone, you know?"

Amy nodded slightly. She looked at the freshly fallen flurries of snow collecting on the nose of her snowboard. "You're wrong, Jimmy. I need to prove it to . . . myself."

Amy wasn't always convinced by Jimmy's charm and good looks. Most girls couldn't resist him. Even at the age of fourteen, Jimmy was a looker. Half American Indian and half Italian, he had black hair, a dark complexion, and piercing blue eyes. Right now, however, none of those attributes were getting him very far.

"This is stupid, and I think —" Jimmy began.

Just then, someone from the crowd let out a shout. "Twenty bucks says she chickens out!"

Amy's brother shook his head and smiled. "You're on, dude," Mark answered. "I know my sister. She may not have any courage, but she's stubborn as heck."

"It's been forty-five minutes, man," another boy said, laughing. "If this takes any longer, we'll be swimming out of here when the snow melts."

Amy's eyes narrowed. She couldn't believe her own brother was betting on her. He was never supportive, never caring. He was usually a big fat jerk, even though she was never anything but nice to him.

That does it, Amy thought. *I'll show them all.*

Pressing her foot forward, Amy dropped in, quickly picking up speed as she shot down the mountain.

Jimmy looked on, dumbfounded. Even though he'd bet on her, he never expected that she'd actually do it.

The crowd rushed to the edge of the mountain, piling on top of one another to watch. At first, Amy's run was as smooth as ice. Then she hit the first set of moguls. She bent her knees, readied her arms, and hit the bumps. Within seconds, she was springing up and down, out of control. Suddenly, Amy was up in the air doing a backward somersault.

Bad idea, she thought, slamming to the ground.

* * *

"Honey?" a voice echoed out into the darkness.

"Amy?" the voice asked again and again.

The darkness faded. Amy opened her eyes and looked up in confusion. Through the haze, her surroundings slowly became clearer. She was home again, lying in her bed, wrapped in her favorite blanket.

Amy's mother, Jessica, sat on the edge of the bed. She stroked Amy's forehead with the tips of her fingers, brushing the long, blond bangs away from her face and out of her crystal blue eyes.

"What happened?" Amy managed to ask.

"Shh," said her mother, giving her daughter a reassuring smile. "You've got a mild concussion, dear."

"But I —?" Amy tried to explain.

"You *biffed*," finished her mother, using her daughter's language to bring out a smile.

Amy's brother Mark stood in the doorway. He casually waved a twenty-dollar bill in the air. "It was glorious!" he finally said. "You popped into the air like a jack rabbit, and then somersaulted down the mountain for a good hundred feet."

"Enough," said his mom, not wanting to hear the details of her daughter's brush with death.

"I was doing so well," Amy grumbled.

"It's okay, baby," said her mother.

"I'm not a baby!" Amy cried out. "And it's not okay! No one believes I can do it. I'm not a coward. I can take on the Falcon any day of the week. It's just —"

"Do you really care what anyone else thinks?" asked her mother.

Amy slowly shook her head. "No," she said. "But I said I could do it, and I'm going to prove it." Amy sat up in bed, trying to leave.

"Whoa, there," said her mother. "I'm sure you're good enough to ride the Falcon, but you don't have to prove anything today, dear."

"You don't believe me either, do you?" cried Amy.

"Sure I do, honey," replied her mother. "Your word is good enough for me."

"Jimmy has seen me do it!" Amy said, not giving up the fight. "I can snowboard really, really well! I just can't seem to do it in front of other people. I get nervous — like I'm going to fail or something."

Amy's mother leaned over and planted a kiss on her daughter's forehead. "I believe you, dear," she said. "Now try and get some rest. I'll check on you in an hour for dinner, okay? Your father will be home then, and he's going to want to check on you, too."

"You told Dad?" shouted Amy. "He's gonna kill me."

Amy's mother just smiled. Then she rose from the bed and pulled the covers under her daughter's chin. "No, he won't, dear," she said. "Your father is just very worried about you."

"The daughter of an FBI agent should have enough confidence to go straight down a hill without getting hurt," Amy mumbled quietly.

"Yes," her mother agreed. "But the daughter of an FBI agent should know better than go trying to prove things to other people — especially when most of those people aren't even her friends."

Amy knew her mother was right, but she wasn't about to admit it.

2

"Mom said you had quite the flight today," said Amy's father, William Kestrel. He took the small bowl of mashed potatoes from his daughter.

William was a traditional man from a large family. His mother had taught him the importance of quality family time. So every night, no matter how hectic things were, the family sat together at the dinner table, catching up on the day's events.

They were a family, a team, a unit, and he wanted them to remember that.

"Uh, oh that —" Amy started.

"It was awesome!" interrupted her brother. "She got so angry when the other kids said she wasn't going to do it. Then she just popped off the mountain!"

Mark threw his hands over his head, waving them in the air like he was flailing and falling. He contorted his face into an exaggerated expression of fear. "You should have been there, Dad," he said, starting to laugh. "It was priceless!"

"So you were there?" William asked his son, his voice low and even.

"Well, sure," began Mark.

William's eyes narrowed into a familiar glare.

"Oh," Mark said, realizing his fault.

"Yeah, 'Oh,'" his Dad repeated, scooping more potatoes onto his plate. "You do know Amy could have been hurt, right? Or even killed?"

"I guess so, but —" Mark started again.

"And you stood there?" his father interrupted. "You didn't try to stop her?"

"How exactly is this my fault?" Mark asked.

"You're her older brother, Mark," explained his father. "You're supposed to help her when she needs it — not make fun of her in front of other people so you look funny or cool."

Mark stammered, unsure of what to say.

Then Amy spoke up in his defense. "It wasn't his fault, Dad," she said. "I did it."

"Yeah! *She* did it!" Mark exclaimed.

"Yes, you did." William's tone changed as he leaned in closer to his daughter and smiled. "How did you do before you fell, huh?" he asked, giving Amy a playful jab on the shoulder.

"William!" shouted Jessica. "Do not encourage her!"

"Don't do that again, young lady," said William and then gave his daughter a quick wink.

*　*　*

"So you're not mad?" Amy asked.

An hour later, William stood at the sink, scrubbing the dishes. Amy dried them off, placed them in the cupboards, and waited for the next one. Another ritual.

"No, not mad," her father said. "Just disappointed."

That little word hurt more than any grounding, spanking, or punishment. Amy's parents meant everything to her. They had sacrificed so much.

Years ago, her mother was just getting used to being married to a special agent for the Federal Bureau of Investigation — bouncing from state to state — wherever William was needed. Then Mark was born. Jessica expected that raising a child and living in that high-stress environment day after day would be impossible.

But soon, she returned part-time to work, and then became pregnant again. This time with Amy.

After graduating from college, William knew exactly what he wanted to do. He joined the FBI. Luckily, his traveling from state to state took a pause when he became Director of Indian Affairs in the Boulder, Colorado office. He was happy for the opportunity. Helping people was something William loved, and he hoped that trait had been passed to his children.

"You're not a braggart. Why did you do it?" William asked, handing Amy another dish to dry.

"We were talking about Four Directions Mountain," she began.

"Oh, Four Directions," her father responded knowingly. "American Indians feel that's a central place for all the energies of the planet — all four corners of the globe — converging in one location."

"Exactly!" Amy exclaimed. "I can always board really well there. I'm talking about butters, blindside 180s, switch 360s, air to fakies —"

"I get it, Amy," William said.

She eyed him, surprised. "Really?" Amy asked.

"I mean — no, I don't," her father continued. "But I understand what you're saying."

"I can't explain it either, Dad," she added. "I really do well out there. I get super-confident, and it's like —" Amy paused for a moment, considering her next words carefully. "— like an electricity moves through me when I'm up there. Dad, I can actually feel a tingle flowing from my toes to my fingers."

"Early people felt that place was full of mystical power," William explained. "Maybe you're drawing from that energy."

Amy placed a bowl into the kitchen cupboard and then turned to look at her father. "You really think so, Dad?" she asked.

"Ever since I started working here, I've heard some pretty strange stories about that mountain," William said. "But I'm not a scientist. Maybe it's just the beginnings of frostbite, for all I know. Besides, what does any of this have to do with what happened today?"

"Some older kids heard Jimmy and I talking about the power," Amy replied. "They called me a liar."

William raised his eyebrows. "Oh?"

"Yeah, they got all mad and were about to start a fight," Amy explained.

"So you said you'd prove it?" asked her father.

"I'm sorry, Dad," she said, drying the last dish from that evening's meal.

William dried off his hands, turned off the sink, and hugged his daughter. He looked down at her, straight in the eyes. He brushed her golden hair away from her face and spoke kindly. "You did what you thought you needed to do to stop a fight," he said. "You protected your friend . . . but you also put yourself in danger. You don't need to prove anything to anyone, honey. You know in your heart that you can do anything you set your mind to. But bragging about it — even if you *can* do it — is wrong. That's not the Kestrel way."

"Yes, sir," Amy said, pulling away and looking down at the floor.

"Okay," William said. "Homework time."

Amy stepped out of the kitchen without saying another word, figuring she'd gotten off easy.

"Oh, and you're grounded, young lady," added her father before she could make it up the stairs.

"What?!" Amy exclaimed.

"No TV, no internet, no texting," William said.

"But, Dad!" she pleaded, looking down the stairs at her father.

William looked up at his daughter and smiled. "For tonight," he added.

Amy ran back down the stairs and gave her father a hug. He understood — even when no one else did.

"Thanks, Daddy," she said in her most loving voice.

"Be glad I'm not your mother," William replied. "She wanted to ground you until you were thirty. Now go read something, will you?"

3

"Grounded for one night?!" exclaimed Jimmy as he met with Amy the next day. "Man, my dad would have grounded me for a whole year."

"Yeah, well, your dad's a Tribal Chief," Amy said.

"And your dad's in the FBI!" Jimmy shot back.

"So they're both tough, but fair," she said.

"True," Jimmy grumbled.

"And at least they like each other," she said.

The morning had brought a short respite in the storm, but the snowfall the night before had slammed the city's roads with freshly packed ice. Crews were working overtime to clear the streets, but none of the schools were open. And, more than likely, they were going to be closed all week.

This was great for the kids, and even better for the ski resorts. Like many others, Amy and Jimmy decided to hit their favorite snowboarding spot.

The pair cut through Warner's Field on their way to the American Indian reservation. Their composite backpacks held their gear: carbon fiber helmets, top of the line snowboards and bindings, and everything else they needed for a full day on the mountain.

Both of them were gear heads. They loved the sport, but they also loved collecting the latest and greatest equipment — the best goggles, the best gloves, and the best hats. Every dime they got from their allowances they spent on gear.

Their fancy outfits were part of the reason that other kids thought they were posers. Most kids in their school didn't really care what kind of gear they used, but Amy and Jimmy felt that expensive gear helped. The gadgets got them hyped up about the sport, boosted their attention, and made them focus on being better athletes.

As they reached the outskirts of the reservation, Four Directions Mountain loomed above them.

"Ready for the hike?" Jimmy asked. He dropped his backpack and started breathing heavily.

Amy smiled at the sight.

"Are *you?*'" Amy said, laughing at her friend.

Truth is, Jimmy was far from out of shape. As the star of the school's track team, the fourteen-year-old was as lean and fit as any distance runner — something Amy had definitely started noticing during the past year.

Though they weren't technically a couple, Amy did have a slight crush on Jimmy. As her best friend, Jimmy was her protector. Not that she really needed one. Still, she knew he'd always be there for her.

Standing at the base of the mountain, Amy took off her backpack, pulled out her goggles, and placed them on the snow. Just then, Jimmy caught sight of a small bag of cookies in Amy's pack.

"Whatever, Little Miss Cookie Monster!" Jimmy joked.

Amy was used to attention from boys. All her life, she'd been that popular girl. In middle school, she was on the drill team, and when she hit junior high, Amy tried out and made the cheerleading squad. She was cute, with her straight honey-blond hair, a button nose, and crystal blue eyes. However, most boys flocked to her because she was kind and sweet, and she never let her in-crowd status make her to treat people differently — something she learned from her parents.

When they entered high school, Amy and Jimmy were being thrust into a new social circle. Kids from all around the county were bussed to one central school. True friends needed to stick together.

Snapping on her goggles, Amy reloaded her pack, slung it over her shoulder, and they moved out again. Above them, as they hiked toward the summit, Amy noticed a white falcon circling overhead. Leaning her head to the side, she watched as the bird orbited them and then flew off, taking exactly the same path they were hiking.

"Well, looks like we'll have another audience today," Amy said, pointing out the bird to Jimmy.

* * *

An hour later, the two friends reached the summit of Four Directions Mountain. Then suddenly, Amy began to feel it — a slight tingling in her toes and fingers.

She grabbed Jimmy's arm and stopped abruptly. "Do you feel that?!" she asked, somewhat frightened.

Jimmy looked down at his arm. "Uh, yeah," he said. "You're cutting off the circulation to my arm."

"No," Amy said, letting go. "The tingling! In your fingers?"

"It's just the cold, Amy," Jimmy said.

"No, I know that's not it!" Amy protested. She detached her snowboard from her backpack and locked into the bindings.

"Altitude sickness? I dunno. Will you just do me a favor today, huh?" Jimmy pleaded.

"What?" she asked.

"Don't overdo it today, okay?" said her friend, concerned. "If that paramedic wasn't there yesterday . . . I don't want to —" Jimmy stopped.

Amy looked at him and smiled. "You don't what?" she asked softly.

"I don't want to —" Jimmy paused again. For a moment, he looked sad, but then the teen let out a little laugh. "I don't want to carry you home on my back through this powder. Seriously, you should lay off those cookies."

Amy backhanded him on the shoulder. "Very sweet, jerk," she said. Then she adjusted the goggles on her nose and took off down the mountain.

Slowly at first, just getting the feel of the run, they moved back and forth down the mountain. Like falling leaves, they cut wispy trails through the fresh powder.

Amy loved how the mountain changed each day. Snow, ice, and wind transformed the speed of any given run and added different elements to its terrain.

Amy and Jimmy also knew that, on any given day, the first time down any slope should be an easy training run. Use the first run to get the "feel" of the mountain, like NASCAR drivers do with a training lap on a new track. Only then, after you've assessed the mountain, could you get tricky with it.

Amy picked up speed.

Spotting her out of the corner of his eye, Jimmy yelled over. "Heelside, Amy! Heelside!"

"I know, I know," she snapped back. Amy dug in the edge of her board and decreased her speed.

Ignoring his own advice, Jimmy picked up the pace. He shot down the mountain, reaching the middle of the 15,000-foot slope rather quickly while taking a visual inventory of the run: rocks, trees, moguls, dips, drifts, and possible jumps.

Suddenly, Amy began to feel the electricity again. The strange crackling power built inside of her body as she sped down the decline. Unable to control it, she stopped, shook out her hands, and flexed her fingers. She tried desperately to get the warm blood circulating through them. But the tingling wouldn't stop and, oddly enough, it didn't hurt at all.

The feeling was like static electricity — every muscle in her body exploded with life.

Amy felt indestructible.

Taking off her right glove, she examined her hands. A small amount of blue electricity arced and swam around her fingers. It jumped back and forth on her painted nails like sparking metal conductors.

Amy's eyes filled with wonder and confusion. She searched for Jimmy. She wanted to show him what was happening, but he was too far away to see. Without him, Amy didn't have anyone to keep her grounded. Her confidence level was at an all-time high. And, at that very moment, Amy Kestrel knew she could do anything she imagined.

Suddenly, a loud cawing from above caught her attention. Amy looked up. The falcon had returned and was orbiting her again. Then, the falcon soared ahead of her. A hundred yards in the distance, the mysterious bird landed on a small snowdrift that looked like a skateboarding ramp made of ice and snow. The bird glared at her and let out a desperate squawk.

Amy's eyes narrowed as she leaned forward.

Grinding to a halt, Jimmy looked back up at Amy as she garlanded down the mountainside. He admired her gracefulness and skill.

Just then, his smile dropped as Amy picked up speed, heading toward a monster jump.

"Uh, oh . . ." Jimmy said to himself.

But Amy couldn't hear his concern. She leaned into her momentum, balled her fists and, like a bullet from a gun, shot faster and faster down the slope.

"No!" Jimmy yelled. He broke out of his snowboard bindings and raced up the hill on foot.

It was too late.

Amy hit the jump, soaring fifteen feet into the air. Snow and ice shot off her board like the condensation trail from a fighter jet. The falcon was following her, trailing the teen through the air.

For Amy, time seemed to slow momentarily. She bent down, twisted her torso, and grabbed onto the edge of her snowboard. Amy blasted through the air, rotating, and executed a perfect Indy 540. Then, as expertly as she had taken off, Amy landed without fault, gliding onto the snow as if she'd been going big her entire life.

Grinding to a halt, Amy bent over and caught her breath. Time returned to normal, and even she was amazed at how perfectly the trick had gone.

Above her, the falcon dipped its wings and shot into the sky.

Jimmy ran up to her with a pale face. He couldn't believe his eyes. "How did you —?"

"I don't know," Amy began. But she didn't get a chance to finish. Suddenly, a massive blast of wind rushed over the mountain crest, almost blowing them both to the ground.

With a lion-like roar, a lone Black Hawk helicopter shot over the ridgeline and hovered into view. With its rotor blades kicking up snow and ice, the aircraft levitated directly above the teens, looming like a robotic vulture.

"You are trespassing in a restricted zone and are in criminal violation!" a mechanical voice boomed down from the chopper. "Do not move!"

Shielding their faces from the flying ice, Amy and Jimmy watched doors slide open on both sides of the chopper. Four spaghetti-like black ropes emerged, uncoiling toward the snow below.

Abruptly, the voice came again. "You will be escorted to the bottom of the mountain," the speakers boomed, "where you will be processed for removal from this area."

Jimmy looked at Amy. "We were just here last week!" he shouted. "What the heck is going on?!"

Amy shrugged. She knew the area as well as anyone, and nothing like this had ever happened before. *Wouldn't Dad have warned me?* Amy wondered.

All at once, four men wearing black uniforms and mirrored helmets appeared at the chopper doors. With skis strapped to their backpacks, they fast-roped down from the helicopter and landed right next to the teens.

Amy yelped with surprise and started kicking away on her snowboard.

"Don't move!'" the first guard ordered. Speaking through the microphone in his helmet, his voice sounded mechanical and raspy. "You're trespassing on restricted ground."

Jimmy looked confused. This area was an Indian reservation. As far as he knew, these men had no authority here.

Jimmy spun and looked the first guard in the face, but was met with his own reflection on the helmet's faceplate. "Trespassing? I live here, man! You're not with the tribal police. I demand —"

Another guard stepped forward, towering over the young boy. He appeared to be the squad's leader. "You are in no position to make demands, *sir*," the man said.

Jimmy was about to get angry, and Amy knew it. She placed a calming hand on his forearm and stepped forward. Amy was anything but new to people in authority and piped up commandingly.

"My name is Amy Kestrel," she said.

"Perhaps you know my father?" she continued. "Special Agent William Kestrel of the *FBI*? I want to call him now."

Amy pulled out her cell phone from her pocket. But before she could make a call, the leader snatched it from her glove.

"Hey!" she protested.

"Miss, I don't care if your dad's the President of the United States. You're trespassing on restricted property," he said. "We're going to escort you and your companion clear of the area. Do you understand me?"

"Yes, sir," she answered. *Maybe this isn't the best place to pick an argument*, Amy thought, recognizing her dangerous position on the edge of the mountain.

The lead guard cocked his helmeted head to the side and chuckled. Then, in a flash, each member removed their skis from their backpacks.

Moments later, they were herding Amy and Jimmy down toward the base of the Four Directions Mountain.

4

During the descent, Amy did what her father had always taught her to do in sticky situations: be as observant as possible.

"If you ever find yourself in trouble," he would say. "Make mental notes. Even the smallest details — license plate numbers, body types, eye color — can help detectives solve a crime."

Amy hoped she wasn't headed into a crime scene today, but she didn't know who to trust. These men looked official. Still, something about them wasn't right. Besides their strange and concealing helmets, the men wore an odd patch on the chest of their uniforms. Amy thought it looked somewhat like the Presidential Seal, an image she recognized from her father's briefcase.

However, instead of an American bald eagle, this seal featured a black and gold hawk. Clutched in the bird's talons — instead of the presidential arrows and an olive branch — were lightning bolts and a sword. In the background, embroidered in red thread, was a globe with three Latin words written across it:

Armis Exposcere Pacem

Whatever that means, Amy thought. Unfortunately, she took French, not Latin, so the meaning was lost on her. However, her father certainly would know, so Amy made mental notes and continued to observe. The squad's uniforms were made of hard materials — leather and neoprene — like what a motorcyclist or someone competing in downhill skiing events would wear. They had utility belts around their waists and black leather pouches filled with who knows what.

Something else about the four men struck Amy as odd. Though they carried a baton type of weapon, none of the men were armed with a handgun or rifle. This was baffling to her because, as far as she knew, none of the agencies that would be authorized to take them into custody would be caught dead without a ranged, defensive weapon.

Even park rangers carry guns around these parts, Amy thought.

As the group slowly made their way down the mountain, Amy looked back at the man following her. She assumed it was the first guard she'd spoken with when they arrived, but the other two looked exactly the same. Only the leader stood out.

"What agency did you all say you were with again?" Amy asked.

"We didn't," the guard shot back. "Now keep moving, Miss Kestrel."

As they came over the ridgeline, toward the Mountain's far facing base, both Jimmy and Amy's eyes widened in surprise. They saw something that had never existed in that space before today.

The entire area looked like something out of the movies. Four main trailers had been moved in to set up a command post between the hundred-foot Douglas firs and pine trees. About fifty men, all in black cold-weather parkas and snow pants, moved about the mountainside conversing, exchanging papers, and surveying the area.

Meanwhile, three giant backhoes were in the process of digging up ditches and removing the tightly packed snow layer. Each hole the machines created was about ten square feet. Several scientists worked inside each pit, scraping the earth with excavating tools.

Surrounding the base of operations was a makeshift perimeter of orange plastic fencing that cordoned off the area from anyone trying to get through. Towers of tall, metal posts lit up the area with dozens of white-hot spotlights.

Amy thought the scientists appeared to be searching for something important. *But what?* she wondered.

This land had been a sacred place to Jimmy's ancestors. Amy could tell he was starting to get very angry. She tried getting his attention, but he was too busy surveying the man-made destruction.

Finally, the group reached their destination. An older man walked up and greeted them. "I'm Dr. Welker," he said to Amy and Jimmy. "Thank goodness we got to you in time. Now let's get you home."

The guards backed off as the man put his arms around the teenagers. He led them away from the trailer, heading toward a break in the perimeter. Waiting there were two black SUVs with knobby snow tires and brush guards. Their engines were already running and ready to go.

"What? Wait —" Amy began, pulling away from the doctor. She turned to face both of the guards, put her hands on her hips, and refused to move. "I'm not going anywhere until you explain all this."

The doctor turned to the squad leader and frowned. "You didn't tell them, Captain Abaddon?" he asked.

The guard silently shook his head.

"As you both know, these are sacred grounds," the doctor explained. "Recently, evidence was unearthed proving there are major archeological finds here — ones that predate even the earliest people. Several specimens of Plesiadapis that link prehistoric man to this 50 million year old primate have been discovered right at this spot. We're trying to uncover this find while still preserving the ancient traditions of this area's native peoples. The entire mountain has been cordoned off as a precaution to anyone damaging or disturbing what could be the most significant find of the decade — the century even!"

"Why would we be in any danger?" Amy asked, still not buying the story.

"The recent snowpack isn't as tight as we'd hoped," continued Doctor Welker. "Any disturbance in the drift could cause a major avalanche."

Amy looked around at the hardware the science teams were wielding. Electronic devices of every kind littered the scene. Different team members utilized everything from sonar scanners to Geiger counters and even electromagnetic radiation detectors.

The scientists had also set up a protective perimeter that not even a mouse could get through. Three towers made of metal spires and antennas shot fifty feet into the air like advanced lightning rods. *No archeological expedition in the world has this much high-tech equipment,* Amy thought.

"And those?" she asked, pointing up at the large metal spires.

The doctor smiled. "Ah, the weather vanes," he said. "Just some sophisticated weather sensing equipment. We have very sensitive scanning tools here, dear, and we'd hate for anything to damage them. Actually, on top of an avalanche threat, there's an electromagnetic storm front coming in that could become very harmful to our group's activities. Got to plan for these things. Always be prepared."

As they neared the vehicles, the rear passenger doors to both SUVs swung open. The doctor nudged Jimmy to the right, toward the open door.

"Please show these fine children back home," the doctor told the driver. Then he turned toward the teens. "Let your friends know that this area is restricted. No more *thrashing* on the mountain, okay?"

"Sure thing, Pops," Jimmy said with a laugh. Then he hopped into the back of the SUV.

Amy stopped for a moment. Then, against her better judgment and the advice of her father, she slid into the vehicle as well. Eyes narrowing, she peered over at the doctor and Captain Abaddon. "And the tribal elders agreed to this excavation?" she asked.

"Oh yes!" said Doctor Welker without hesitation. "They were very accommodating!"

"I doubt that . . ." Amy mumbled under her breath, and then started to close the vehicle's door.

Just then, Captain Abaddon reached up and grabbed the frame, stopping the door from closing. Amy gazed at her reflection in the man's helmet, staring at what she thought would be his eyes.

"Yes, Captain?" Amy asked politely.

"Don't forget this, Miss," he said. From a pocket on his utility belt, the captain pulled out Amy's cell phone. She quickly took it, thanked the squad leader, and shut the door.

As the SUVs drove off, the doctor's demeanor drastically changed. His face went from all smiles to a deep, ingrained scowl. "Captain, I want you to keep an eye on them," he said. "A very close eye."

5

"All of their permits are in order, Chief. Someone gave approval for them to excavate in these parts," said William Kestrel. He spoke with Chief Thomas Parker, Jimmy's father, at the Bureau of Indian Affairs.

"Agent Kestrel —" Parker stopped and then started again. "Bill, we've known each other for a long time. Heck, our kids are practically dating."

Kestrel smiled at that.

"But I'm telling you," he continued, "the Tribal Council didn't agree to these actions. These people are on our land illegally."

William nodded. He knew that any archeological digs on the reservation had to be cleared with the council, but everything appeared to be in order.

"I understand, Thomas," said Kestrel, throwing up his hands. "But what can I do? They have the council's approval seal on their paperwork."

"It's a forgery," Parker proclaimed.

"And I believe you," said Kestrel. "But I can't ride in there and throw 'em out without investigating it first. Neither can you. To register a formal protest, I need you and the other leaders to put it in writing."

"More bureaucracy," Parker scoffed.

Kestrel's voice became more serious, less personal. "My official recommendation," he said, "and this is just a suggestion: Let the archeologists do their thing and get out of here as quickly as possible."

Parker shook his head and shot a piercing look at his childhood friend. "They scared our kids, Bill," he said. "They used four men and a chopper to force our kids off that mountain. Doesn't that seem a little over the top to you?"

Kestrel turned and looked out his office window. In the lobby, Amy and Jimmy sat and waited near the secretary at the front desk. They both looked a little frazzled and exhausted by the day's experience.

Kestrel frowned. "Trust me, I'm not happy either," he said. "I've already contacted the lead scientist, but he's not giving me solid answers."

"Who are they?" asked Parker, growing more and more frustrated. "The kids said the site looks like some sort of government operation. They said the scientists have blocked off access to the mountain. Can't you check them out on the computer, or something?"

"This isn't the movies, Parker," Kestrel replied. "We're not all interconnected, but I've already made a few inquiries. So far, everything's come back negative on the government side. This group's obviously corporate, privately owned. But it's weird —" He looked through a stack of papers on his desk. "Besides their website and a few tax statements, this group doesn't seem to exist."

Chief Parker looked defeated.

"Don't worry," added Kestrel, trying to reassure him. "I'll keep checkin. And I'll be sure to keep you in the loop."

"I appreciate that, Bill," said Parker. "I've always trusted you."

"I wouldn't have it any other way, Thomas," he replied. "And, like I said, get me that formal complaint. I'll see what I can do."

The men shook hands. Then Chief Parker walked out, collected Jimmy, and left.

Still sitting in the lobby, Amy looked at her father, searching for answers as well.

"Let's go home," said Kestrel, recognizing the concern in his daughter's eyes.

Amy followed her father out of the Bureau offices, through the parking lot, and into the family's four-door sedan. For a while, they drove over the freshly plowed streets in silence. The snow began falling again, and the headlights from the car reflected like prisms off the icy flakes.

"So who are they?" Amy finally mustered the courage to ask.

"Honestly, I don't know, honey," answered her father. "Do you remember anything more about these men?"

"Of course, Dad," she replied. "How many times have you told me to —"

"— keep mental notes," they both said at the same time.

"Yes, well," said her father, not amused by the coincidence, "I've also told you to *never* get inside a strange vehicle."

"I know, Dad," Amy confessed. "It was stupid. But everything looked so legit. They had an official emblem."

"An emblem?" asked her father.

"Yeah," she said, "like the Presidential Seal, you know? With the Latin and everything."

"What did it say?" he asked.

Amy struggled to remember. "I dunno," she replied. Armed — Armed Expose — Pac-Man?"

Kestrel glance over at his daughter and couldn't help but smile. "Pac-Man?" he said with a laugh.

Amy laughed as well.

"What else can you remember?" her father prodded.

"Well, the helicopter was like the one Uncle Barry flies for the Army," she said.

"A Black Hawk?" Kestrel said.

"Yeah," said Amy. "But the chopper didn't have any markings on it. No numbers. Just black like their uniforms."

Amy turned and looked out the passenger side window. She tried to piece the information together herself, but nothing made any sense.

"That screams private corporation," Kestrel mumbled under his breath. "But even they should have tail numbers on an aircraft like that."

Amy wasn't focused anymore. Her mind kept drifting back over the events of the day, especially what had happened before the helicopter shot over the mountain and the strangers appeared. She'd almost forgotten about her amazing jump, about that mysterious electric energy, and about the falcon.

Or was it even a falcon? Amy thought.

Ticking off her mental notes about the bird's appearance, Amy became convinced it was a kestrel, the bird that shared her family name. She was also convinced that the mountain was trying to tell her something. Something magical. Something powerful.

But no matter how understanding her father could be, he was still a man of logic. And, although he had an understanding of the mythical, he always tried to find the rational explanation to the problem at hand. That was his job, after all. It's what he did for a living. Still, Amy couldn't leave out any details about the day.

"Dad?" she asked.

"Yes, dear?"

"Something else happened on the mountain," Amy started, working up the courage to tell him.

"What?" he asked.

"I felt it again," she finally said.

"What? The electricity?" her father asked.

Amy nodded. "It was stronger this time. Different."

"What do you mean 'different'?" Kestrel asked.

"The energy —" she paused again. *What would he think?* Amy wondered. *Would he think I was crazy? Would he just dismiss it? Would he try to convince me of alternative explanations?*

"The energy arced across my fingertips, Dad," she said. "I could feel my body tingling."

"What are you talking about, Amy?" asked her father. "Did those men taser you kids or something?"

"No! Remember what I told you before? The energy?" said Amy. "This time, I felt it flow through all of my muscles. And then, when I took off my glove, there it was! I'm not kidding, Dad, blue electricity shot across my fingertips. Oh, and then this falcon showed up and circled us. I mean, it wasn't a regular falcon, but the bird could have been a kestrel —"

"Slow down, Amy," her father interrupted. "Did you say you saw a kestrel?"

Amy nodded. "Yeah, why?" she asked. "Don't you think seeing the electricity is a little more unusual?"

Her father's eyes narrowed. He looked at Amy and slowly held up his hand. Suddenly, William Kestrel slowed the car and pulled to the side of the road. Then he shifted the car into park and faced his daughter.

"Years ago, on the day you were born," he began, "Chief Parker told your mom and I that you were special. He said the elders had come to him. They had foretold that you would deliver something wonderful to the world. And this great wonder would come on the wings of a falcon."

The blood ran out of Amy's cheeks.

Her father continued. "He told us that the kestrel would come like lightning and show you a path to greatness."

Amy's eyes went wide. Her heart race as she looked at her father in amazement. "What — what does that mean, Dad?" she asked him impatiently. "What am I supposed to do?"

"I dunno, sweetie. Your mother and I have been trying to figure that out for years," her father replied. "However, many of this land's early peoples believed in magical spirits that bound them to animals. They considered them totems. Birds were especially important and powerful. For you to recognize that power on your own is —"

"What?" Amy interrupted.

"Amazing," concluded her father.

"And what does the mountain have to do with all this," she asked, searching for more answers to the day's mysteries.

"Good question," said Kestrel. "And one to ponder later."

"Later?" Amy protested.

"I want you to listen to me," her father said, locking eyes with his daughter. "I mean, really hear me."

"Okay, Dad," said Amy, recognizing the importance of his next words.

"Don't go back to Four Directions Mountain," he said. "Until I figure out the motives of these scientists, I don't want you nosing around out there. It's not safe. That goes for Jimmy as well. Understood?"

Amy looked her dad square in the eyes and nodded. "Yes, sir," she answered.

"Okay, then," Kestrel said. He shifted the car into drive, and they headed toward home once again.

Amy frowned and sunk back into her seat. She had just told her father a bald-faced lie.

6

Early the next morning, Amy and Jimmy Parker
trekked across the base of Four Directions Mountain
once again. This time, however, the light of the moon
and the stars was guiding them — not a falcon.

"I can't believe we're doing this," Jimmy mumbled
under his breath.

"I can hear you," said Amy, turning toward her
friend and pointing toward the summit. "And I have to
find out what's happening up there."

"I care about the mountain too, you know?" said
Jimmy. "But —"

"Then come with me," she said, turning to continue
their trek through the icy snow. "And stop your
whining."

Even this far off, Amy and Jimmy could already see the giant metal spires sticking out of the mountain's forest of pine trees.

Amy stopped again and pointed at the towers. "Last night, I searched the Internet for anything that looked like that equipment," she said.

"And?" questioned Jimmy.

"The closest image I could find was a high-tech military scanner," replied Amy. "They're looking for something, all right —"

"Duh," Jimmy blurted out.

"Would you let me finish, hot shot?" shouted Amy. "They're looking for something with an energy source — like electricity or radiation."

"Radiation?" Jimmy squeaked. "Dude, I'm not going to lose my hair, am I?"

"I'm serious, Jimmy," she said. "Don't you see? This has to be linked to that mysterious energy I've felt out here recently."

"Yeah, so?"

"So we're going to find it first," said Amy.

"Wait, wait, wait . . . let me see if I've got this straight," Jimmy began, sounding concerned. "You want us to summit this mountain in the dark, locate this power source, and outsmart a military SWAT team?"

"Yep," stated Amy.

Jimmy laughed. "You're something, all right," he said. "Just tell me one thing. Why? Why risk so much for this little thing?"

"You didn't feel it, Jimmy," she explained. "I felt unstoppable — like I could shoot lightning from my fingertips. I felt alive!"

"Okay," said Jimmy. "I get it."

"Then what's the problem?" she asked.

Jimmy grabbed Amy's arm and looked her in the eye. Even though she was closer to Jimmy than any other person her age, Amy rarely felt him touch her. She liked it, but would never admit that fact.

"I don't want you to get hurt," Jimmy said softly.

"*Whatevs* —" Amy said, trying to pull away from his grasp. He wouldn't let her go.

"I'm serious, Amy," said Jimmy, pulling her even closer. "I don't — I don't want you to get hurt."

Amy could feel Jimmy's breath on her face. Despite liking him more than any other boy, she had never thought about kissing him until now. *Now's the time*, she thought. Amy batted her eyes and inched a little closer with anticipation.

Then suddenly, just like the day before, Amy heard a loud crowing overhead.

She looked toward the sky. The kestrel had returned, circling fifty feet above them. "There!" Amy shouted. "Do you see it?

Jimmy looked up in a daze. "Stupid bird . . ." he mumbled to himself.

"It's him, Jimmy," Amy exclaimed. "My totem!"

"How do you know?" he asked skeptically.

Instinctively, Amy stuck out her arm. The large bird immediately rocketed toward the teen. Jimmy ducked for cover, but Amy stood still, somehow knowing the bird meant her no harm. A split second later, the kestrel landed, its talons gently wrapped around Amy's delicate forearm.

The bird swiveled its massive neck, looked Amy straight in the eye, and let out a tremendous squawk.

"Whoa!" said Jimmy, completely stupefied.

"Now do you believe me?" Amy said with a smirk.

Jimmy simply nodded.

"Somehow, this creature and I are connected," Amy wondered aloud. She slowly reached up and gently rubber her forefinger on the kestrel's beak.

"Then maybe it knows where to go," added Jimmy.

Amy smiled. "Do you?" she asked the bird. "Do you know what they're looking for? Do you know what I'm supposed to find?"

Without a sound, the bird launched into the sky, circled once, and flew off toward the summit.

"I'll take that as a 'Yes,'" Amy shouted, and ran after the bird. "Come on, Jimmy!"

The boy shook his head and followed closely behind.

An hour later, a hundred yards from the summit
of Four Directions Mountain, Amy and Jimmy stopped.
They spotted what looked like the same guards from
the previous afternoon, and quickly ducked for cover.

One of the men carried a strange piece of equipment
in his arms, which looked like a high-tech metal
detector. He swept the machine's scanner across the
ground, obviously searching for something beneath the
thick base of snow.

"What do you think?" one of the guards asked the
other as he continued sweeping the ground.

"Personally, I think the Old Man has lost his
marbles," another man answered. "This is a wild goose
chase, if you ask me."

"How so?" asked the man with the scanner.

"The pieces, the key, the kids . . . it's all a huge waste of time," replied the other guard, slumping onto a rock and taking an unauthorized break. "The Old Man should learn a little from history, you know?"

Amy and Jimmy remained hidden only a few yards away, listening carefully. Hands clasped over their mouths, they didn't dare breathe. Even the vapors of their warm breath in the frigid air would give away their position to the guards.

"Why don't you tell him that?" said the guard with the scanner. "I'm sure the Old Man would love to hear your opinion."

"Yeah, right," the other guard scoffed.

"Then stop whining," the guard ordered, "and get back to work."

"Hey," interrupted a third guard with a thick, frosted beard. "At least the Old Man is paying us this time. Not like when we were in Afghanistan or Somalia, right?"

"Yeah, I guess so," replied the lazy guard, rising from the rock. "I just think we could be doing so much more."

The guard with the scanner looked down at his wrist. A small computer strapped to his forearm gleamed back at him.

"It's almost two o'clock," said the guard. "If we skip this sector and hustle back on skis, we might make it back in time for late chow." Then he dropped his pack and unstrapped his skis from their harness.

"Let's do it!" echoed the other guards.

Each squad member pulled two wands from a pouch in their utility belts. Pressing the buttons on either side, a pair of ski poles telescoped out from each of them.

Amy eyed their gear. *I have to get me some of those,* she thought.

Then, in a flash, the men rocketed down the mountain and disappeared into the night.

Standing, Amy gazed after them. *Afghanistan? Somalia? Dad was right! Those men are soldiers for hire,* she thought. *But who was this "Old Man" they were talking about, and what was the "key"? Is that what they were looking for?*

"So, what now?" Jimmy asked as he stood and wiped the snow away from his chest.

"Look —!" said Amy, pointing into the sky. The mysterious bird zoomed through the air and came to a halt about 100 yards away. It perched on a snow-covered tree limb, calling out to the teens.

"Isn't that the jump you took this morning?" Jimmy asked Amy.

A huge smile crept across Amy's face. "Come on!" she shouted, running in the direction of the bird. As she got closer, her hands and feet began to tingle, and Jimmy noticed her excitement.

"Feeling that energy again?" he asked.

"Oh yeah," she said, picking up speed and pulling ahead of him.

As they closed in on the bird, the sensation got stronger, more intense. Finally, Amy dropped to her knees, removed her pack, and fished around inside.

"What is it?" Jimmy asked.

Amy's hands emerged from the pack, wrapped around a small entrenching tool. As she snapped its shovel blade open, she looked up at her friend.

"It's here!" Amy said, frantically digging into the thick layer of snow.

"If you say so," said Jimmy. He helped her dig, using his gloved hands to plow through the powder.

As they dug deeper and deeper, the kestrel became more and more excited. It shrieked wildly until — *clunk!* Finally, Amy's shovel hit frozen dirt.

"Here, let me," Jimmy offered.

He took the shovel from Amy, stood, and put his foot on the top of the blade. Then he began chipping away at the solid earth below.

Jimmy was growing tired, but he tried not to show his fatigue.

"My big, strong man," Amy joked.

Embarrassed, Jimmy's face turned red. He looked away from her, concentrating on the job at hand.

Shovelful after shovelful of frozen brown soil clumped together with thick slabs of ice came up from the small two-foot diameter hole. Then, suddenly, the shovel made a *thunking* sound.

Jimmy looked at Amy with excitement. She didn't hesitate. Reaching inside the hole, Amy fished around until finally —

"Got it!" she exclaimed.

With suspense, Jimmy waited to see what Amy had in her hands. His pulse quickened. His eyes widened in anticipation. Then, as the items broke the lip of their small crater, his face dropped into a confused, contorted scowl.

"What are they?" Jimmy said, puzzled.

In her hands, Amy had two small pieces of splintered wood, each no bigger than a slice of sandwich bread. On one side of them, there was a small section of what looked like worn-out sandpaper, sheered, ripped, and full of holes. On the other side, there were some markings, like part of a painting of an Iron Cross.

But more importantly, the small bits of electricity Amy had been experiencing were now in direct contact with her skin. The energy in her hand began to crackle and pop. A small field of blue electricity swam around her fingers.

Amy felt a sudden burst of current race through her. All at once, she was supercharged. Her muscles were energized, and she felt like she could take on the world.

"I don't know what this is, but I like it . . . !" she said, letting out a wild-eyed laugh.

Amy stood, and the blue electricity flowed through the wood pieces, down her arms, and through her legs. Jimmy reached out to grab the mysterious fragments.

"Hey!" said Amy, not wanting to let go.

"I'm not trying to take it, Amy," said Jimmy, "but I think I recognize that image."

Amy turned the pieces over so Jimmy could get a better look at the mysterious markings. He stared at the graphic. Butting up to what remained of the Iron Cross was what looked like an artist's rendition of a skullcap.

"I know what these are!" Jimmy proclaimed.

"You do?" she replied, stunned.

"They're parts of a skateboard!" Jimmy declared.

"What? Skateboards are made of wood. And wood isn't a conductor of electricity," she argued.

Jimmy reached into his pack and pulled out one of his skateboarding magazines. He flipped through the pages, searching frantically for a specific image.

"Right there!" he shouted, finally stopping on a full-page picture of a skateboard.

And there it was, clear as crystal. A vintage Tony Hawk skateboard — the same exact model he had used to compete in the 1999 X Games competition. Amy couldn't believe what she was seeing.

"Can I look now?" Jimmy asked, holding out his hand toward the pieces of the board.

"Sure," Amy began, sticking one piece in her utility belt and preparing to give Jimmy the other.

Just then, a rustling of air above them drew their attention. Out of the sky, like a dive-bomber, a dark brown hawk descended on them. In an instant, the hawk had snatched one piece of the board in its talons and bolted into the air.

"Hey!" Amy yelled after the aerial predator.

Nearby, the kestrel took off like a jet, racing after the other bird. It sped through the sky, caught up to the hawk, and swiped at the intruder with its beak. Caught by surprise, the hawk lost its grip on the piece of skateboard. The kestrel darted after it, catching the piece in midair. Mission accomplished.

Streaking through the air like a blur, a small nylon net surrounded the kestrel. The bird plummeted toward the earth.

Looking on in horror, Amy cried out as the kestrel lost its grip on the fragment and continued tumbling toward the ground. *Fwump!* The bird hit the ground and was buried in a thick pile of snow.

Jimmy looked up, and saw the skateboard fragment falling right toward him. He raised his hands. Then, suddenly, a black leather glove reached up and intercepted it, ripping the piece from the air right in front of Jimmy's face.

"I'll take that," a mechanical voice growled.

Jimmy turned and saw Captain Abaddon standing beside him, holding the fragment in his hand. Flanking him on either side were the guards. One of them held a smoking net-gun in his hands.

The captain placed the piece of board into the largest pouch on his utility belt. Then he turned his attention to Amy. She was cradling the fallen kestrel in her hands. It was still alive but severely injured.

Amy unwrapped the bird from the netting. Without hesitating, the kestrel hopped up and looked around. It squawked, alerting its savior to the man standing beside her in the snow.

"Evening, Miss," said the captain, reaching out and offering his hand to Amy.

Gripping his leather glove, Amy stood peering into the black abyss of his helmet. "How did you know we were here?" she asked, patting the snow off her clothing.

Then, without asking for permission, Captain Abaddon dug his hand into Amy's jacket pocket.

"Hey!" she exclaimed.

Before she could pull away, the captain yanked out Amy's cell phone and held it up for her to see. Pulling the battery cover off the back, he removed a small chip that wasn't supposed to be there.

"A tracking device," he said, closing the phone's case and handing it back to her. "We've known your whereabouts since you left our custody yesterday."

"Mercenary," she answered.

The captain laughed and turned to the guards. "Let them go," he ordered.

A moment passed, but the guards did not obey the command.

"Did I stutter?" shouted the captain. "I told you to let these kids go!"

"Uh, sir?" one of them said. "I don't understand. They know of the Fragment's existence."

The captain rolled his eyes. "Well they certainly do now, don't they, Corporal?!" he exclaimed, clearly agitated by the incompetence of his inferiors.

As the men argued back and forth about what to do with them, Jimmy decided it was time for action. Getting Amy's attention, Jimmy glanced up at the guard next to him, then over to her, and then nodded down the mountainside.

Immediately, Amy understood. She readied herself for action.

"The standing order from the Old Man is to remove anyone who has seen or has immediate knowledge of the Fragment's existence!" the guard protested. His voice grew louder, and he pulled his baton from its sheath. He pressed the activation button and a small purple electrical field began to glow at the tip. Then he approached Jimmy.

"Stand down, Corporal," Abaddon commanded, but the corporal kept moving toward Jimmy.

"I said stand down!" the captain yelled again. This time, the guard listened. He turned off and holstered his taser baton. Both men were now within striking range of Jimmy's position.

And that's exactly where Jimmy wanted them!

Thwap!

Jimmy kicked out his leg and struck one of the guards in the back of the knee. The guard buckled. He hit the powder hard, grabbing at his leg and moaning in pain.

In a flash, Amy was up, her bag in hand, and she was heading toward the summit.

Meanwhile, Jimmy turned his attention to the corporal. He tripped him to the snow. Then, jumping on top of the guard, Jimmy tussled and tried to keep him on the ground. He threw elbows and punches the best he could.

Meanwhile, Amy made a run for it. She glanced back to see that Jimmy was not right behind her as she had thought. He was involved in a grappling war with both guards.

"Jimmy!" she called. Unfortunately, this got Captain Abaddon's attention as well.

"Go!" Jimmy hollered between punches as he rumbled with both men.

She couldn't. Amy couldn't leave him there to face all three of them alone, but when Captain Abaddon turned to give chase, she knew she had to go.

Dropping to one knee, the captain grabbed up the net-gun and reloaded it. He aimed at the center of Amy's back . . . and fired. *Bang!*

The shot went wide.

To Amy's left, the capture net slammed around the trunk of a pine tree. Amy was safe. *For now,* she thought.

Finally at the top of the run, Amy locked into her bindings and popped onto the slope. Her snowboard chewed up the mountain. She was bombing the beast — no tricks, no turns — just doing what she could to get out as fast as she could.

Looking over her shoulder, Amy thought that the coast looked clear. But when a clump of snow fell from above her, she knew something was wrong.

Looking up, Amy got a glimpse of a pair of black skis, backlit by the silver light of the moon, sailing off a jump above her.

With a slam, the corporal landed next to her!

8

Darkness and quiet surrounded Amy. After eluding the corporal, she had taken refuge in a shallow cave on the far side of Four Directions Mountain. She wrapped her arms around her legs, trying to keep warm as the moon moved higher and higher into the sky.

An hour had passed since her amazing getaway, but it felt more like days. She was freezing and wondering where to go next.

Who are these guys? she kept asking herself. *Why are they here? What do they want from me? They kept mentioning pieces of a key — key to what?*

Overcome with emotion, Amy's eyes welled up with tears. She thought about poor Jimmy, all alone, being held by those mercenaries.

Amy couldn't believe what she had done. She had abandoned her best friend in the whole world. But she needed to get away. Otherwise, both of them would have been in a sticky situation.

Now what? What was she going to do? If she went back out there, a roving patrol or the helicopter might pick her up. That wouldn't do either of them any good. She needed a plan.

Amy knew she could always call her dad. He'd come in with the FBI, and who knows what kind of violence that would start. There might be some kind of standoff, and Jimmy could get hurt. Or even worse.

No, she needed something different — a distraction, maybe. She needed something that would enable her to get in, free Jimmy, and recover the other fragment of the skateboard without getting caught in a fight.

And what is that thing? Amy wondered. How could a piece of a broken skateboard — if that's what it was — conduct electricity? And what was it doing to her?

Amy shook her head. All of those details would have to wait. Right now, she needed to come up with a strategy . . . and fast.

Amy thought about her situation. *What would be the best distraction?* Then an idea came to her like a bolt of lightning. She opened her phone and dialed.

* * *

It was three in the morning, but Mark Kestrel was still awake, sitting at his computer. He and several of his snowboarding pals were playing an online adventure game when he saw his cell phone light up on the desk next to him.

On its screen, Mark saw his sister's number flashing.

"Sorry, guys, hang on a sec —" he growled into his gaming headset and then picked up the phone.

"What?" Mark asked, annoyed that she'd interrupted his online quest. "You're calling me from your room now? Too lazy to walk downstairs?"

"Mark?" Amy's voice interrupted. The reception was terrible and full of static, like she was miles away.

"Amy?" Mark asked again. "Seriously, what —?"

Cradling the phone to his ear, Mark stood up, walked out of his room and down the hall. Whispering, he opened Amy's bedroom door quietly, so as not to wake their parents. Peering inside, he was surprised when he saw Amy wasn't in her room.

Mark stepped inside and shut the door. All of a sudden, Mark was in serious big-brother mode. "Where are you?" he demanded.

Her voice told him that something was wrong.

"I'm —" she began, her voice shivering from the cold. "I'm in trouble and need help."

"I'll get dad," replied Mark.

"No!" she cried. "I need your help, Mark."

"Me?"

"Yes, you," Amy begged. "And your friends."

Mark looked at the floor for a second, ran his hand through his hair, and finally nodded.

"We going to get in trouble?" he muttered.

"Probably," his sister replied.

Mark smiled. "Then count me in."

* * *

Meanwhile, at the base of Four Directions Mountain, Jimmy sat tied to a metal chair in the scientist's mobile command center. He was locked in a small office, lights off, and all alone. Only a crack in the blinds covering a plate-glass window gave him a hint to what was happening in the rest of the trailer.

Jimmy struggled to see clearly. Squinting hard, he was able to make out several men in lab coats moving on the other side of the glass. In the center of the room, he saw what looked like a small surgeon's table bathed in fluorescent lights.

After a few moments, Dr. Welker entered the room. He held a small metal box, cradling it like a baby in his arms. Then, setting it down on the examining table, Welker took a step back. He began speaking and gesturing wildly with his hands.

Jimmy struggled to hear, but no sound was getting through the glass. It was obviously soundproof — and sealed from the outside.

Reaching over, Dr. Welker opened the box as the other scientists gathered around to see. Inside, sitting in a lining of densely packed foam was the skateboard piece Amy and Jimmy had found.

Jimmy grunted. He struggled to see more, but he finally slumped down in the chair, realizing there was nothing he could do. Leaning his head back against the headrest, Jimmy sighed.

He didn't know what was going to happen to him now. Would they let him go? Would they remove him like the corporal wanted? Luckily, Amy'd gotten away, so, hopefully, she'd come back with help soon.

Suddenly, the lights in the room went from white to red. An alarm rang out through the compound. Looking up, Jimmy could see confusion had filled the observation room. Dr. Welker was doing his best to keep everyone calm.

Unable to control his guards, Dr. Welker rushed outside, stumbling from the trailer so quickly he forgot his parka. Helmeted guards were scurrying in every direction. They readied their defensive equipment, and the science team scuttled for cover.

"What's this all about, Captain?!" Dr. Welker shouted at his security commander.

Hoisting a net-gun into the air, Abaddon turned to the doctor. He shook his helmeted head from side to side. "We're not sure," he said. "There are several blips on the aerial radar. They could be incoming choppers, or maybe —"

Just then, several air horns blasted loudly into the sky — the attacker's planned warning signal.

Dr. Welker and Captain Abaddon turned toward the sounds. A hundred yards up the mountainside, ten snowboarders and five snowmobiles — swishing and grinding down the slopes — headed straight for them like heat-seeking missiles. They blasted into the encampment, wearing ski masks that completely covered their faces.

The other scientists poured out of the observation lab. A group of well-prepared guards escorted them to the two Black Hawk helicopters, which were readying for takeoff.

The snowboarders zipped past them in every direction. The mystery riders hurled rock-filled snowballs at the cockpits as the pilots skipped through their power-up sequence and hurried to go.

Several of the boys flew off of jumps and gouged paint and dented metal as they landed nose slides and 50-50's onto the hoods and roofs of vehicles. Car alarms blared. Lights flashed. But the boys kept on going, laughing at the damage they'd done.

Other boys threw rocks like major-league pitchers at the compound windows, causing glass to crack and splinter as they bounced off the bulletproof surfaces. Others launched backside 720s off the roofs of the trailers, thoroughly enjoying the experience.

Snowmobiles ripped past the guards at their perimeter. They pulled powerslides as they turned, drenching the guards and scientists in cascades of falling snow.

Several of the boarders brandished bats and hockey sticks, ripping down the slope like kamikaze pilots. They struck at the scientific equipment, knocking over weather vanes, smashing lights, and causing havoc.

Everywhere the guards turned, snowboards or snowmobiles flashed by them at dizzying rates of speed.

Eyes wide in shock and awe, Dr. Welker shrieked, "Who are those kids?!"

Captain Abaddon simply shook his head. "I have no idea, sir," he replied calmly.

"Well, figure it out, Captain!" commanded Dr. Welker. "That's what I'm paying you for!"

9

Meanwhile, as the raid on the compound continued, no one seemed to notice Amy. She had quietly traversed the backside of Four Directions Mountain and crept to the entrance of the main science trailer.

She opened the door and quickly ducked inside.

The room was dimly lit by flashing red alarm lamps that flickered on and off. Amy was almost blind in the room, but she knew she was on the right track because her hands began to tingle.

Then, she spotted it. Sitting on a small metal table in the center of the room was the lead-lined box that she instantly recognized.

As Amy slowly moved toward it, she knew exactly what was inside.

Amy's hands shook as she slowly reached out for the box. Taking it up, she felt whole again, completely confident and secure.

* * *

"Corporal!" the doctor yelled, still trying to get the raid under control.

Out of the mayhem, the corporal appeared and ran to them. He gave the doctor a quick salute.

"Yes, sir?" asked the corporal, ready for action.

"I'm going to gather my things," stated Dr. Welker. "Secure the Fragment on Chopper One, and then take care of the prisoner."

"With pleasure, sir," replied the corporal.

"And you, Captain!" said the doctor, turning to Abaddon. "Take control of this situation. We're gone in thirty minutes! No traces." Without waiting for an affirmative, Dr. Welker headed toward the main trailer.

* * *

Meanwhile, inside the trailer, Amy continued searching until something caught her eye. She turned slowly, stunned at the sight before her.

"Jimmy!" Amy whispered.

If the situation hadn't been so dire, the image of Jimmy struggling, bobbing up and down in the chair would have been hysterical.

But now wasn't the time for laughter. Amy quickly ran to her friend's side. "Oh, my gosh!" she nearly screamed, pulling at the zip ties that bound her friend to the chair. "Did they hurt you, Jimmy. Are you okay?"

"No — I'm mean, yes. I'm fine," Jimmy replied, watching Amy struggle with the restraints. "What are you doing here? What's all that noise?"

Amy didn't answer. She continued struggling with the plastic restraints, but her best efforts failed. She couldn't break them with her bare hands.

Amy placed the lead-lined box on the floor and removed her trusty backpack. Reaching inside, she pulled out a mountain climbing tool, and then snapped open the rope cutter.

As she was about to cut Jimmy free, Amy froze. A familiar voice echoed out of the darkness behind her.

"Aren't I lucky . . . ?" the voice said.

Amy turned to see the corporal standing in the doorway, brandishing his taser baton.

"I think we have a score to settle, little girl," he said, slapping the baton in his hand over and over again.

"If you touch her —!" shouted Jimmy.

"Don't worry, kid," interrupted the corporal. "You're next."

Whump! Before he could finish his sentence, the corporal's body crumpled to the floor.

Amy and Jimmy stared in disbelief. Standing over the body of the corporal was Captain Abaddon. "We have to go!" he said bluntly. "Now."

"We're not going anywhere with you," protested Amy, moving to protect Jimmy.

"Look, we don't have time for this nonsense," the captain tried to explain.

"Who are you?" Amy demanded.

Reaching up, the captain unlatched the clasps on either side of his helmet and — with a *whoosh* of air — pulled it off.

Underneath the helmet, a young man's face was revealed. He had a tan complexion, strong jaw, and dark, almond eyes. A small crop of buzz-cut hair that was a bit spiky in the front but shaved on the sides topped his head.

"My name is Warren Rafe," the captain said plainly. "I'm here to help you."

"Bull!" Jimmy exclaimed.

"No, wait —" Amy protested.

Amy stood and cautiously walked over toward
the stranger. Looking up, she stared at the man, deep
into his eyes. "That's why you missed me up on the
mountain," said Amy. "You could've captured me with
that net-gun, but you let me go."

He nodded. "I never miss."

"But why?" Amy asked, confused. "Who are you?"

"I'm from an organization that's trying to stop these
people from getting their hands on the pieces of the
Key," Rafe explained. "You, Amy Kestrel, and those
Fragments are part of that Key."

"I still don't understand," said Amy.

Rafe bent down and retrieved the box from the floor.
Jimmy's eyes narrowed for a moment, but then softened
as soon as Rafe handed the box to Amy.

"Guard those Fragments with your life," Rafe
commanded. "One day they may save you." Then the
captain turned and started toward the door of the
trailer. "Now, let's go!"

As Amy and Rafe started running for the exit, a
sound stopped them dead in their tracks.

"Ahem!"

They turned to see Jimmy, still tied to the chair,
looking a bit miffed. "Forgetting something?" Jimmy
announced loudly. "Or should I say, some*one*!"

* * *

At the same time, outside the trailer, the guards were hustling the scientists into SUVs. The twin helicopters had prepared for liftoff.

On Chopper One, Dr. Welker waited for the corporal to return with his Fragment. He squealed with excitement, knowing the Old Man would be just as pleased. The piece had taken years to locate, and the plan to extract it had been his. Returning with a piece of the puzzle would mean great things for his future.

As the morning sun began to rise, the scientists had little time to wait. The snowboarders were still wreaking chaos in the compound, and one of the massive light towers was about to topple onto the chopper's tail section. On the ground, the kids were repeatedly taking turns slamming their bats into it like lumberjacks downing a massive tree.

"We have to go, sir!" the pilot screamed at Dr. Welker through his headset.

"Not without the corporal!" said the doctor.

"If that tower takes out our tail," the pilot explained frantically, "*none* of us will be leaving!"

Across the compound, the door to the main trailer opened. The doctor spotted Rafe and the teens exiting the building together.

"No!" Welker shouted.

"That's it! We're outta here," the pilot said as he pulled up on the collective stick.

The Black Hawk rose into the air, creating a blast of rotor wash, which blew the snowboarders to the ground. But, the damage had already been done.

"Timber!" one of the boys yelled as they rolled out of the way.

The tower began to fall just as the chopper took off. It slammed into the snow, missing the tail section by mere inches.

Both choppers, carrying the science team and most of the guards, were airborne and flying off into the morning sky.

Hustling to get the kids to safety, Rafe was suddenly grabbed from behind.

"Not yet, traitor!"

Rafe spun just in time to block an incoming roundhouse from the corporal. Rafe countered with a lighting-fast set of jabs to the man's ribs, causing him to stagger.

"Get in the truck!" Rafe ordered Jimmy and Amy as he continued fighting off his attacker.

Rafe thrust his arm out, inviting a counter move. The corporal obliged, but this time, Rafe was ready.

Rafe caught the corporal's fist in his palm, snagging his hand, and in a flash spun him around, flipping the man to the ground. With a super-fast strike, the corporal was out cold. Again.

"And stay down!" Rafe yelled.

Grinding to a halt next to the truck, one of the snowboarders ripped off his mask and looked around.

"Amy!" Mark yelled.

She turned and jumped into her brother's arms, squeezing him tightly.

"Thank you, Mark! Thank you!" she exclaimed.

"Hey, I'm your big brother. It's my job," he replied.

Rafe ran up and smiled at Mark. "You did this?"

"Yep," Mark replied.

"Not bad, kid," Rafe told Mark. "But let's wrap things up and get out of here."

Clipping out of their bindings, several of the snowboarders jumped into the back of the SUV. Others hung on to the rails of the snowmobiles being towed behind.

The remaining guards gave chase, but there was nothing they could do. They could only watch as the young heroes broke free of the perimeter and made their escape — the rising sun glaring off the white, blinding snow on the horizon.

10

Later that afternoon, several official FBI and Colorado Police Department vehicles made their way to the base of Four Directions Mountain.

As they stopped where the previous night's disturbance had occurred, the vehicles popped open their doors. Several police officers, FBI agents, Amy, Jimmy and Mark leaped out. The teens were followed by both of their fathers.

Jimmy ran a few feet, and abruptly stopped. "No, no, no!" he yelled.

"Are we in the wrong place, Amy?" Mark asked, totally confused.

Wide-eyed, Amy slowly shook her head. She looked around, completely dumbfounded.

Amazingly, there was nothing there.

The area was completely as it should have been. No sign that anyone, especially a military-esque compound, had ever been there. The equipment was gone. The holes were filled and covered with fresh snow. The debris from the clash of snowboarders and guardsmen was nowhere to be found.

The area was immaculately undisturbed.

Even Chief Parker couldn't believe his eyes. "Bill, I swear to you —" he began.

William Kestrel just shook his head and placed a consoling hand on his friend's shoulder. "I believe you, Thomas," he said. "Trust me." He looked down at the teens. "And I believe all of you, too."

"But who were they?" Mark asked.

"They're called the Collective," a voice answered from behind them.

The group turned to see Warren Rafe climbing out of a Jeep, followed by two younger men. The first one was about six feet tall with black hair and was wearing a heavy parka. He looked to be about fifteen and not too fond of the cold. The other boy jumped out of the back seat, landing in the snow feet first. He was even taller, with long blond hair, a cocked baseball cap, and a crooked smile.

Pointing his finger in the air and swirling it around in a circle, William Kestrel gave his men the signal to "mount up and move out." Both FBI agents and the police officers loaded into their vehicles. In an instant, the only people left on Four Directions Mountain were the Kestrels, the Parkers, and the three newcomers.

"All right, kid," Kestrel started. "Who are you, and what the heck happened here?"

Smiling, Rafe looked over at his two companions and introduced them. "This here's Omar Grebes."

"Pleasure, sir," the teen with the parka said. He stepped forward and shook Kestrel's hand.

"And this is Dylan Crow," said Rafe.

The other boy shot a disapproving look over to Rafe and raised two fingers into the air at the crowd.

"Call me Slider," he said, winking at Amy and grinning.

Amy smiled.

"And you?" Chief Parker asked.

"I'm Warren Rafe," the man explained. "We're members of a team called the Revolution."

"The what?" Amy asked.

"The Revolution," Rafe repeated. "We're essentially a reconnaissance team made up of some of the best athletes in the world —"

"So, what is it?" William asked. "Some kind of promotional thing for a sporting event?"

"No, sir," Omar interrupted. "Definitely not."

William Kestrel crossed his arms over his chest, waiting for an explanation.

"Let me put it another way," said Rafe. "We're the opposite of the Collective. What they're doing could be extremely destructive to the people of this planet, and we're trying to make sure that doesn't happen."

"The Fragments," Amy said. "There are more of them, aren't there?"

Rafe smiled. "Exactly," he said.

"Fragments?" her father asked. "What Fragments? Kid, you better start breaking this down really fast before I haul all your butts in!"

"The Collective is a secret society of very wealthy and powerful individuals positioned all over the globe," said Rafe. "They're an organization which acts as a shadowy power behind the throne, if you will, using whatever means necessary to achieve their goals."

"*Armis Exposcere Pacem*," Omar said.

"That was it, Dad! Pac-Man!" Amy said excitedly.

"It means —" Omar began.

"Demanding *peace by force of arms*," Kestrel interrupted him.

"Exactly, sir," said Rafe. "Allegedly, they've been the controlling faction for several geopolitical events and world affairs, using their influence in present day governments and corporations to personally benefit themselves. They're believed to be the masterminds behind events that will lead to an establishment of a New World Order."

"A New World Order in their image," Omar stated.

"Yeah, and that'd be bad," Slider blurted out.

"And what does my sister have to do with all this weirdness?" Mark asked.

"Amy's a conduit," said Rafe. "A portal for something we can't really explain yet. She is one of several people, like Omar and Dylan —"

Slider raised an eyebrow.

"— excuse me, Slider," continued Rafe. "We call them Keys. We're not sure how many people are out there who can harness the energy from what we call the Fragments or artifacts."

"You mean, the pieces of the skateboard we found on the mountain?" Jimmy asked.

"Our fear is," said Rafe, "if the Collective assembles all the Fragments and unlocks their power, there'd be no stopping what they could do."

"And you?" Kestrel asked the strangers.

"We're the *anti*-Collective," Omar chimed in. "Under the protection of our founder, we use our cover as a sports team to travel the world in search of the Fragments. We're attempting to stop the Collective from achieving their goals."

Kestrel nodded. He'd heard rumors of an organization like this floating around law enforcement circles for years, but he'd never seen any evidence of its existence ever come to light — until now.

"Your skills on the snowboard were amazing, Amy," Rafe said.

"Pffft!" Mark snorted.

"No, man, it's really true," said Jimmy.

"Each Fragment somehow allows each Key to hone its power, channeling that small amount of energy into them, enhancing their natural abilities to almost super-human heights," Rafe explained.

Mark's jaw dropped as he looked over to his sister.

"Told ya!" She smiled.

"Not only would we be honored to have Amy on our team as an athlete, but she'd be doing the world a great service, Mr. Kestrel," said Rafe.

Chief Parker looked at William, and then nodded over at Amy. "Looks like the prophecy's come true, old friend," he said.

Kestrel smiled. "Can't stand in the way of prophecy, can I?" he said.

"You mean I can go?" Amy asked excitedly.

William Kestrel held up a quieting hand to his daughter and looked at Rafe. "Are there teachers? I mean —" he started.

"Yes, sir," said Rafe. "It's just like training for the Olympics."

"Except with danger and excitement and all that!" Slider interjected with a laugh.

Omar rubbed a hand over his frustrated face. "Dude, shut up," he muttered under his breath.

Rafe reeled to recover. "All the adult chaperones are completely qualified instructors."

"And what do you teach?" Kestrel asked.

"Quantum mechanics, philosophy, and Mixed Martial Arts." He stopped, knowing he'd gone too far.

Kestrel raised an eyebrow and smiled.

"Uh, for those who *want* to learn MMA, that is," Rafe added.

"Okay, everyone in the car!" Kestrel said. "You three." He pointed at Omar, Slider, and Rafe. "Meet us back at our house."

They all sprinted to the sedan — except Jimmy. He stayed behind, looking somewhat saddened.

Chief Parker could tell that all of this wasn't sitting too well with his son. Putting an arm around Jimmy's shoulder, he smiled down at him and pulled him tight. "There's a very old saying that I think applies here, Jimmy," he said.

"Of course," Jimmy said, rolling his eyes.

"If you love something, you have to set it free," said his father. "If it comes back, it's meant to be."

Nodding, Jimmy looked over at Amy as she opened the front door to the sedan. She was saying something to her father, something he couldn't hear, but Bill nodded an affirmative.

Not only was she his best friend, but Jimmy really, truly cared for her. He really did love her, and he was going to miss her.

"And what if it doesn't come back, Dad?" he asked softly.

The Chief sighed. "Give it time, son," he said.

Suddenly, Amy stopped, looked over at them, and smiled. "Chief Parker?" she asked.

"Yes, Amy?"

"Can Jimmy come over for dinner tonight?" she said.

Jimmy looked up at his Dad and smiled.

"Well, I guess I'm on my own with the ice cream tonight," the Chief said as Jimmy laughed.

"Sure thing, Amy!" he yelled back.

"Amy!" Omar shouted.

She spun and looked at her new friend with a child-like wonder. "Yes?" she asked.

Omar, Slider, and Rafe greeted her in unison with her new code name. "Welcome to the Revolution, *Banshee*," they said.

AMY KESTREL_
CODE NAME: BANSHEE

AGE: 14

HOMETOWN: Telluride, Colorado

SPORT: Snowboarding

INTERESTS: Clothes, Gear, and Travel

BIO: Fourteen-year-old Amy Kestrel is a powder pig. Often hidden beneath five layers of hoodies, this bleached blond CO ski bum is tough to spot on the street. However, get her on the slopes, and she's hard to miss. Shredding since the age of three, Amy's well-to-do parents support her ambitions both emotionally and financially. She's always got the latest and greatest gear — custom boards, top-of-the-line boots, and killer shades. Unfortunately, Amy lacks one thing — confidence. At Breck, Telli, or A-Basin, you'll often find her hiding in the pow-pow instead of showing off in the terrain park. But get her alone on the slopes, and she'll prove that posh apparel doesn't make the boarder. It's all about going big and going bold, much like her idols Kelly Clark and Shaun White.

STORY SETTING: Mountains

LOCATING...

ABOUT TONY HAWK

TONY HAWK is the most famous and influential skateboarder of all time. In the 1980s and 1990s, he was instrumental in skateboarding's transformation from fringe pursuit to respected sport. After retiring from competitions in 2000, Tony continues to skate demos and tour all over the world.

He is the founder, President, and CEO of Tony Hawk Inc., which he continues to develop and grow. He is also the founder of the Tony Hawk Foundation, which works to create skateparks and empower youth in low income communities.

TONY HAWK WAS THE FIRST SKATEBOARDER TO LAND THE 900 TRICK, A 2.5 REVOLUTION (900 DEGREES) AERIAL SPIN, PERFORMED ON A SKATEBOARD RAMP.

ABOUT THE AUTHOR_

M. ZACHARY SHERMAN is a veteran of the United States Marine Corps. He has written comics for Marvel, Radical, Image, and Dark Horse. His recent work includes *America's Army: The Graphic Novel, Earp: Saint for Sinners,* and the second book in the *SOCOM: SEAL Team Seven* trilogy.

ABOUT Q & A_

Q: WHEN DID YOU DECIDE TO BECOME A WRITER?

A: I've been writing all my life, but the first professional gig I ever had was a screenplay for Illya Salkind (*Superman 1–3*) back in 1995. But it was a secondary profession, with small assignments here and there, and it wasn't until around 2005 that I began to get serious.

Q: HAS YOUR MILITARY EXPERIENCE AFFECTED YOUR WRITING?

A: Absolutely, especially the discipline I have obtained. Time management is key when working on projects, so you must be able to govern yourself. In regards to story, I've met and been with many different people, which enabled me to become a better storyteller through character.

Q: WHAT OTHER PROJECTS HAVE YOU WORKED ON?

A: I've written several comic projects for companies like Marvel Comics and Image Comics, but I've also written screenplays for several movie projects that are this close to being made into films. And of course, video games like *SAW, Rogue Warrior,* and *America's Army.*

TONY HAWK'S 900 revolution

TONY HAWK'S 900 REVOLUTION, VOL. 1: DROP IN

Omar Grebes never slows down. When he's not shredding concrete at Ocean Beach Skate Park, he's kicking through surf or scarfing down fish tacos from the nearest roadside shop. Soon, his live-or-die lifestyle catches the attention of big-name sponsors. But one of them offers Omar more than he bargained for . . . a chance to become the first member of the mysterious 900 Revolution team and claim his piece of history.

TONY HAWK'S 900 REVOLUTION, VOL. 2: IMPULSE

When you skate in New York, it's all about getting creative, and fourteen-year-old Dylan Crow considers himself a street artist. You won't catch him tagging alley walls. Instead, he paints the streets with his board. He wants to be seen grinding rails in Brooklyn and popping ollies at the Chelsea Piers. But when Dylan starts running with the wrong crowd, his future becomes a lot less certain . . . until he discovers the Revolution.

QUEST CONTINUES...

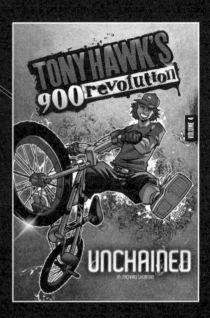

TONY HAWK'S 900 REVOLUTION, VOL. 3: FALL LINE

Amy Kestrel is a powder pig. Often hidden beneath five layers of hoodies, this bleach-blonde, CO ski bum is tough to spot on the street. However, get her on the slopes, and she's hard to miss. Amy always has the latest and greatest gear. But when a group of masked men threaten her mountain, she'll need every ounce of the one thing she lacks — confidence — and only the Revolution can help her find it.

TONY HAWK'S 900 REVOLUTION, VOL. 4: UNCHAINED

Joey Rail learned to ride before he could walk. He's tried every two-wheeled sport imaginable, but he's always come back to BMX freestyle. The skills required for this daring sport suit his personality. Joey is an outdoor enthusiast and loves taking risks. But when he's approached by the first three members of the Revolution, Joey must make a decision . . . follow the same old path or take the road less traveled.

UNCHAINED

. . . Joey Rail looked at his surroundings. Though the rain had washed away much of the evidence, he could get a pretty clear picture of what had transpired. Broken tree limbs, several sets of footprints, tire skid marks from Omar's BMX bike leading to the edge of the cliff.

Omar Grebes was in trouble.

"How many are there?" Joey said quietly.

"What?" Omar asked.

"It looks like about five people were chasing you on foot, and got the drop on you here," replied Joey. He pointed at a nearby bit of undergrowth where the footprints were deepest. "Then they forced you to swerve, and that's when your bike went airborne."

Omar sighed and then smiled. "You're not going to believe me —" he began.

"Try me," interrupted Joey.

"Fine, but we have to move," Omar ordered as he began to hobble off.

"Dude, the way back down is this way," said Joey.

"Yes, but I'm going up," replied Omar.

They trekked toward the plateau of the mountain. It was the exact opposite direction of civilization and the medical attention Omar needed.

"Why, man?" asked Joey. "Tell me what's going on!"

"The Revolution isn't just a sports team," Omar started. And for the next fifteen minutes, he told Joey the story of the team, their origins, and their purpose.

He explained to him about the Artifacts, the Keys and the other sect, the Collective, who was fighting for control of the pieces.

Joey listened as they continued along the path. He could barely believe the tales of supernatural energies, global conspiracies, and international adventure.

Finally, as they reached the end of the man-made trail, Joey stopped and turned to his newfound friend. "What are you doing out here?" Joey asked.

"Searching for the next Fragment," Omar said. He reached into his left cargo pocket and removed a handheld GPS receiver. On it, crosshairs locked in on the North American continent, and then zoomed within three miles of their location — the crest of the summit.

"No way we're climbing, bro," exclaimed Joey.

"Not we," said Omar. "*You.*"

Read more about Joey Rail in the next adventure of ...

Tony Hawk's 900 Revolution

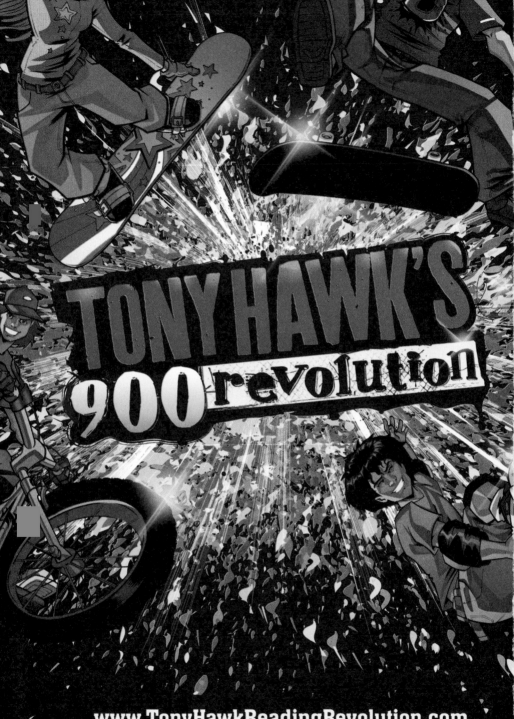

www.TonyHawkReadingRevolution.com

BOCA RATON PUBLIC LIBRARY, FLORIDA

3 3656 0581854 6

J

(Tony Hawk's 900 revolution
 ; v. 3)

NOV   2011